Color by Number

All Things That Move

Color by Number Activity Book

Children's Early Learning Books

BABY PROFESSOR
EDUCATION KIDS

Speedy Publishing LLC
40 E. Main St. #1156
Newark, DE 19711
www.speedypublishing.com

You will have so much fun coloring these vehicles that you won't realize you're practicing important skills like color and number recognition.

Let's get started!

Color the picture using the code below.

1 2 3 4

Color the picture using the code below.

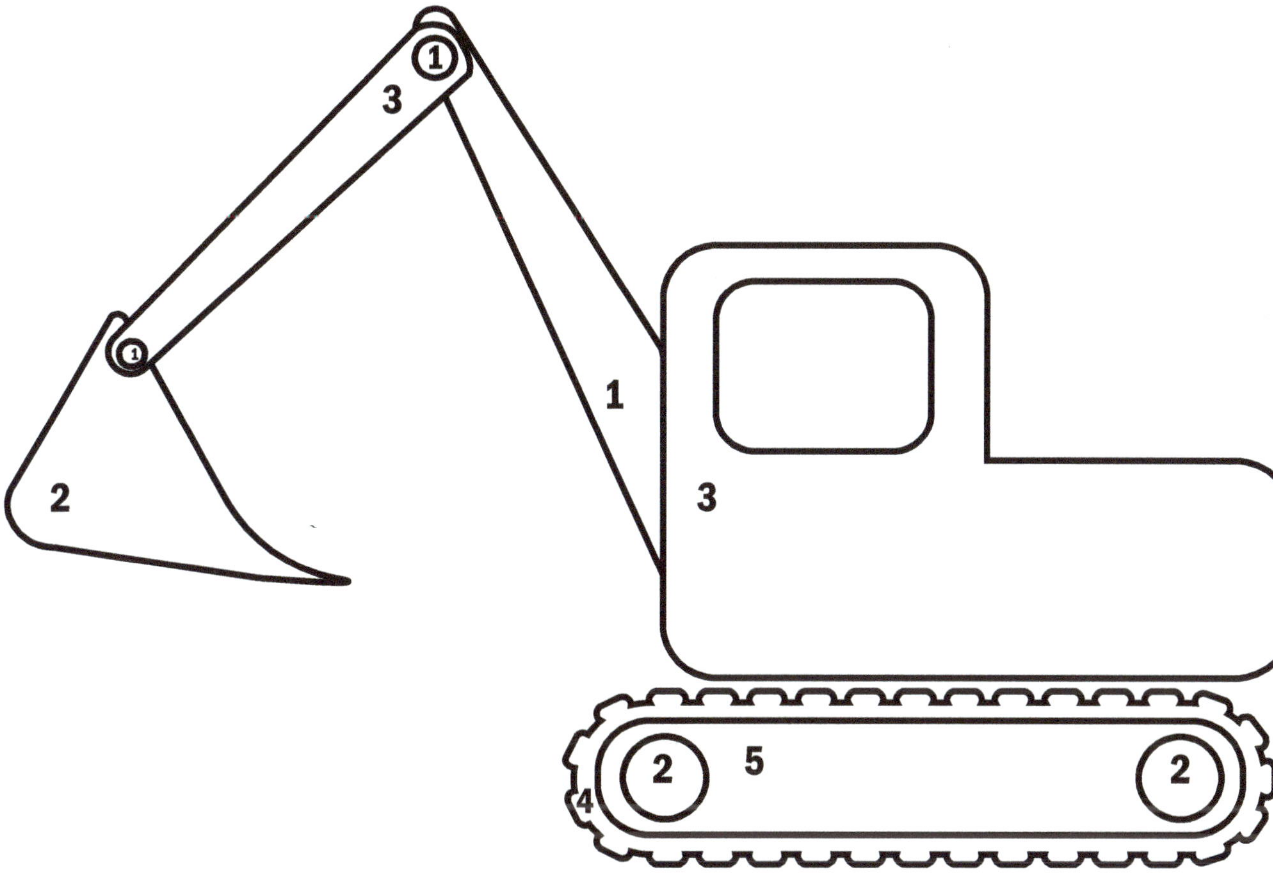

1 2 3 4 5

Color the picture using the code below.

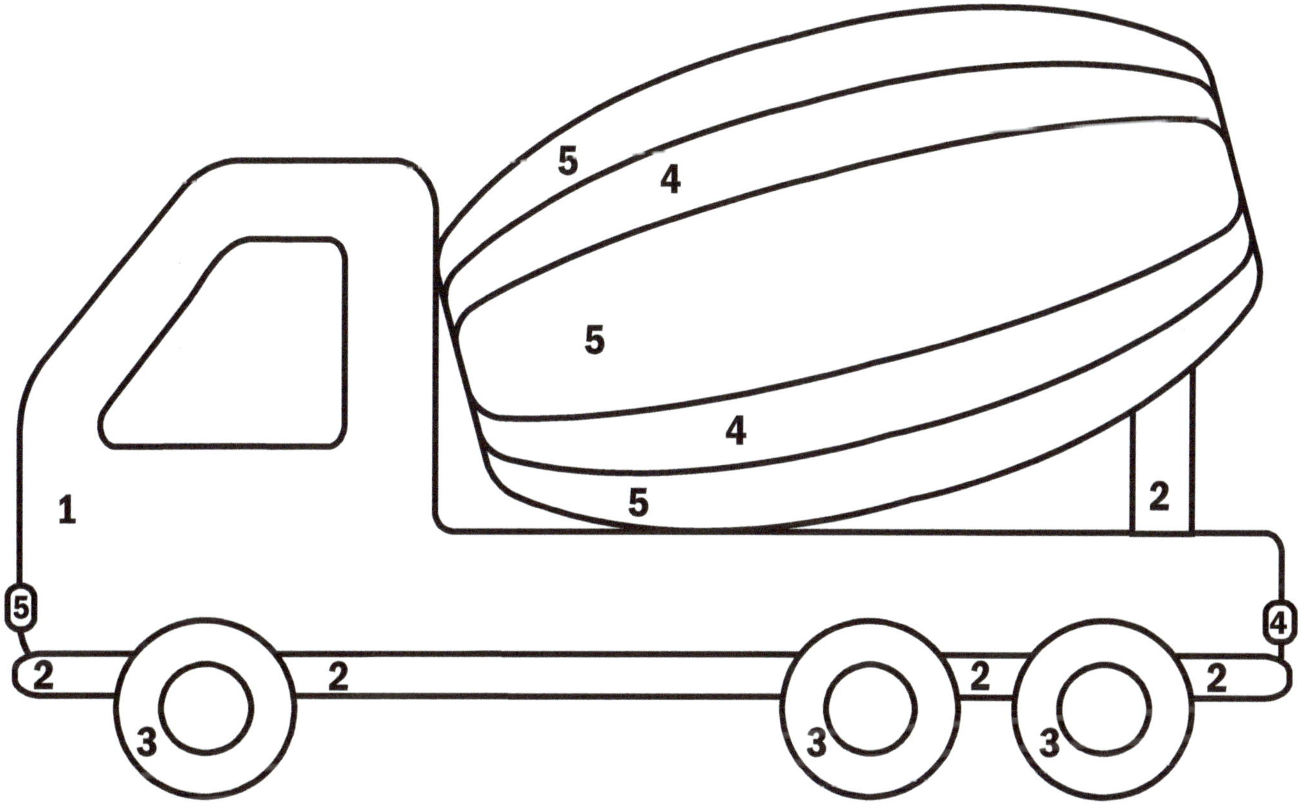

1 2 3 4 5

Color the picture using the code below.

1 2 3 4

Color the picture using the code below.

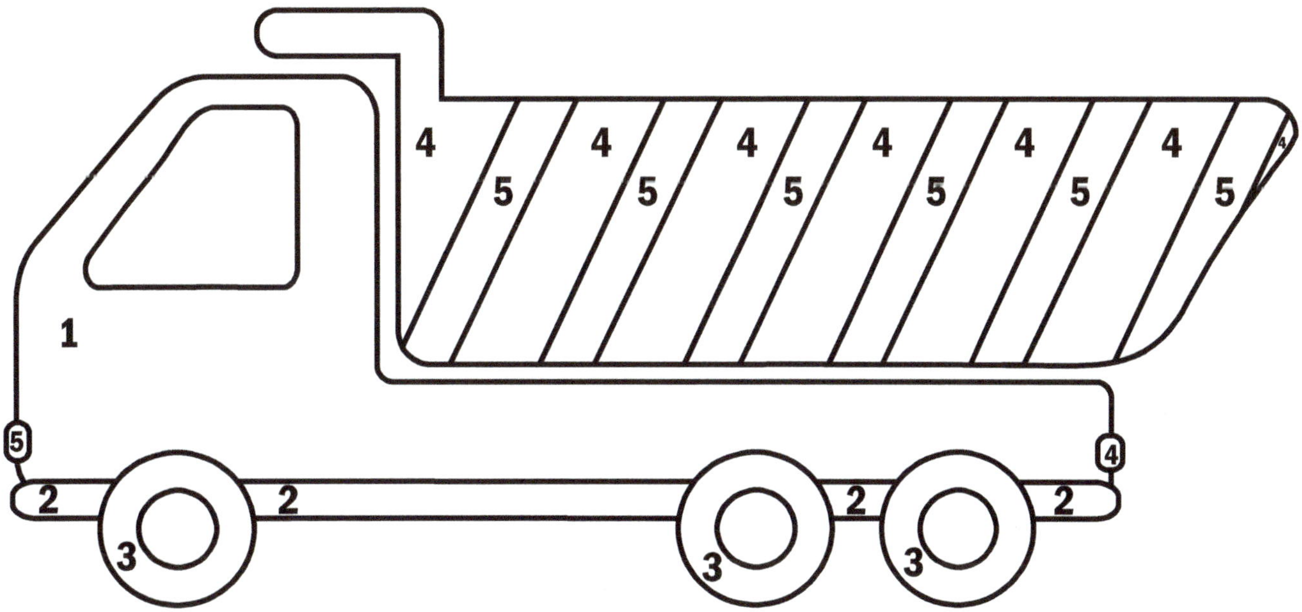

1 2 3 4 5

Color the picture using the code below.

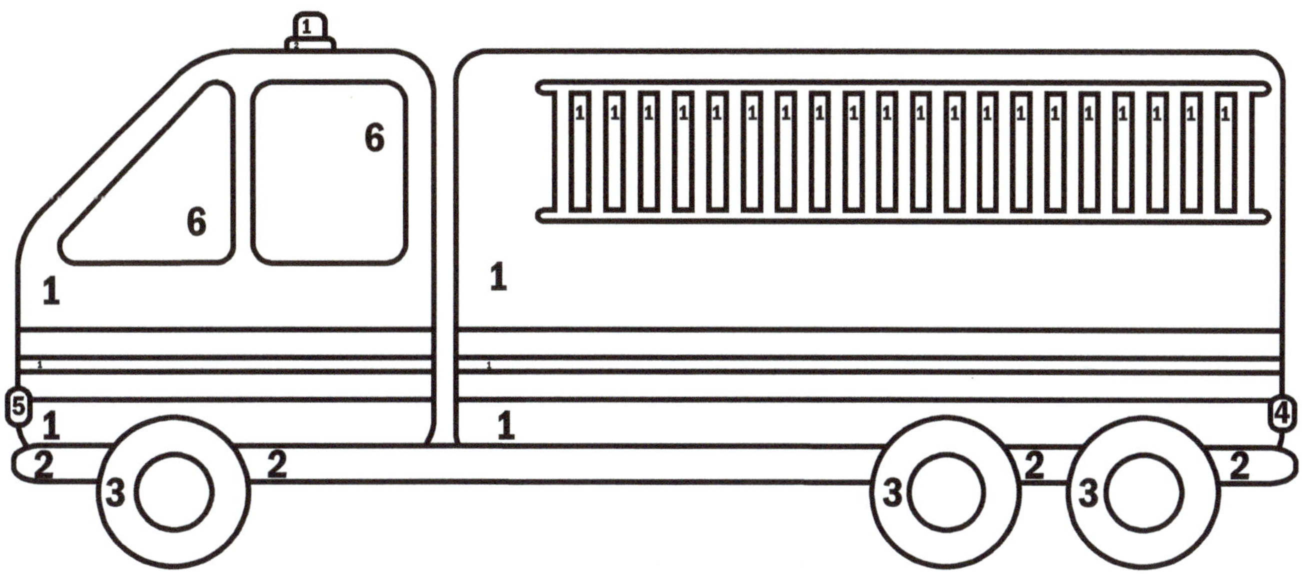

1 2 3 4 5 6

Color the picture using the code below.

Color the picture using the code below.

1 2 3 4 5

Color the picture using the code below.

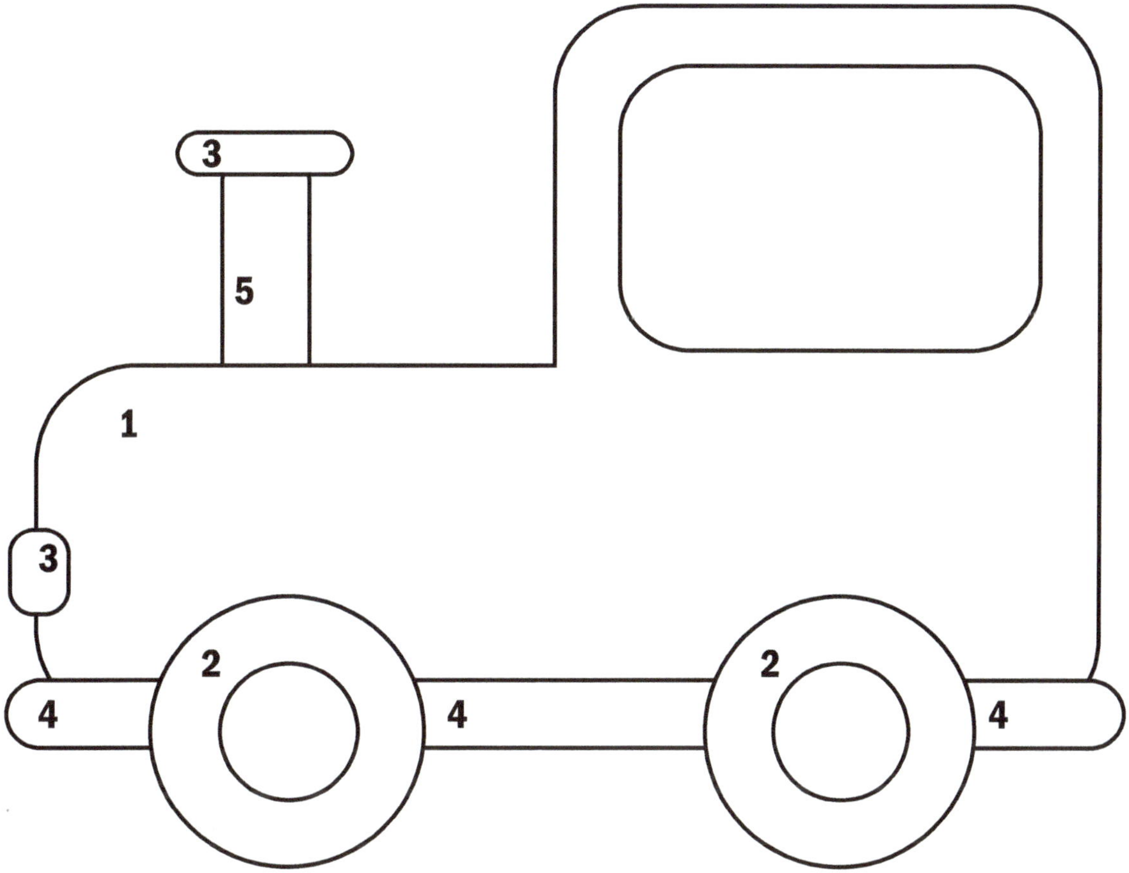

1 2 3 4 5

This is a Bleed Through Page If You Are Using a Coloring Marker or Pen!

Find Other Great Titles By searching for Baby Professor on Your Favorite Book Retailer

Amazon.Com | Barnes & Noble (BN.Com) | Books A Million (BAM.Com)

Color the picture using the code below.

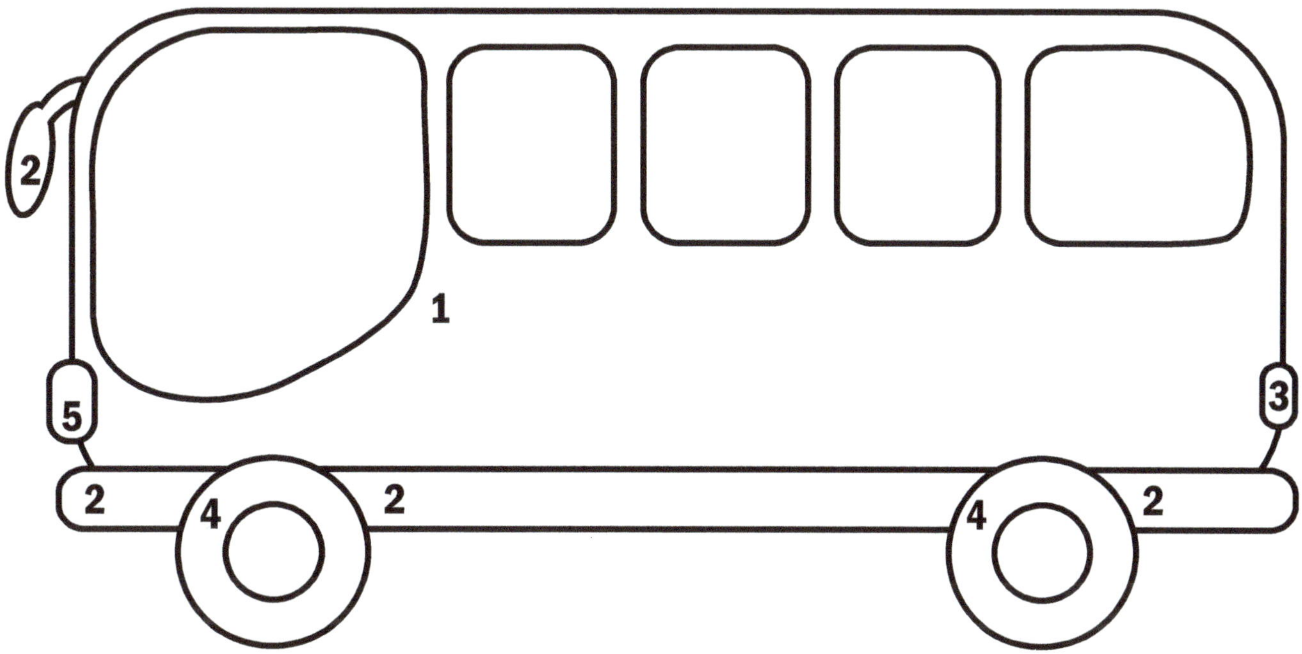

1 2 3 4 5

This is a Bleed Through Page If You Are Using a Coloring Marker or Pen!

Find Other Great Titles By searching for Baby Professor on Your Favorite Book Retailer

Amazon.Com | Barnes & Noble (BN.Com) | Books A Million (BAM.Com)

Color the picture using the code below.

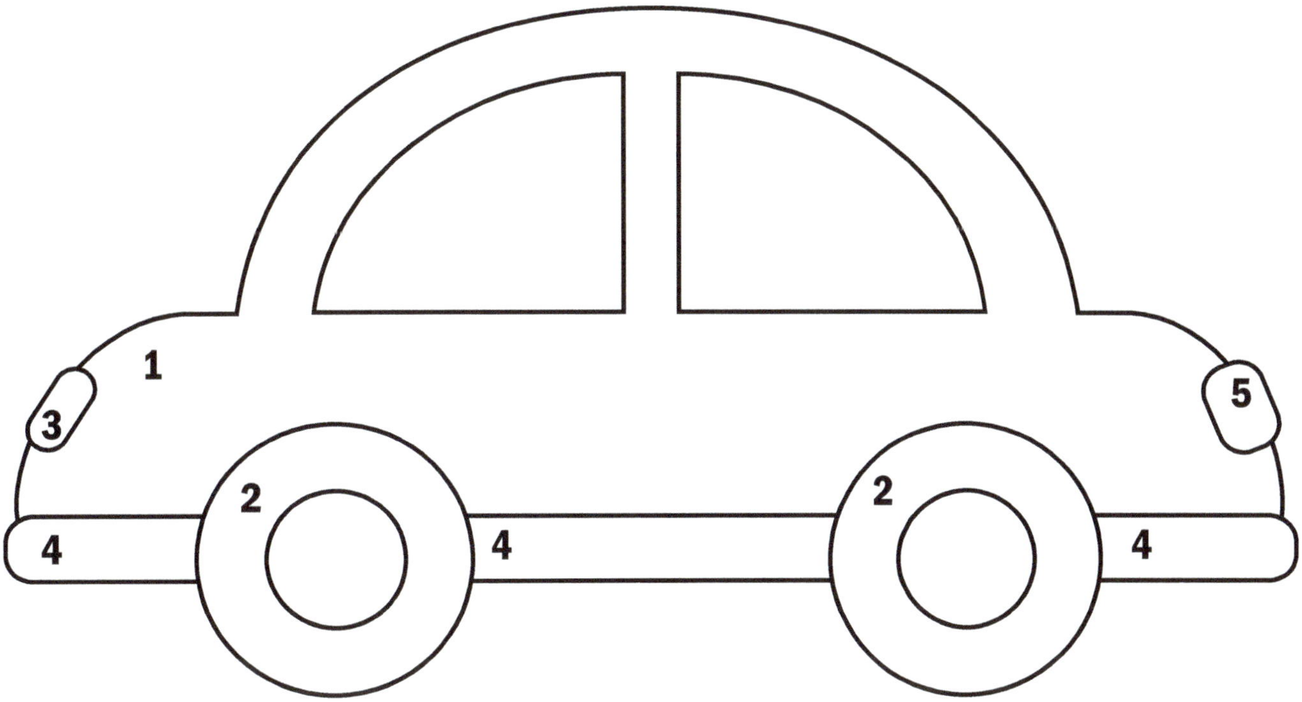

1 2 3 4 5

Color the picture using the code below.

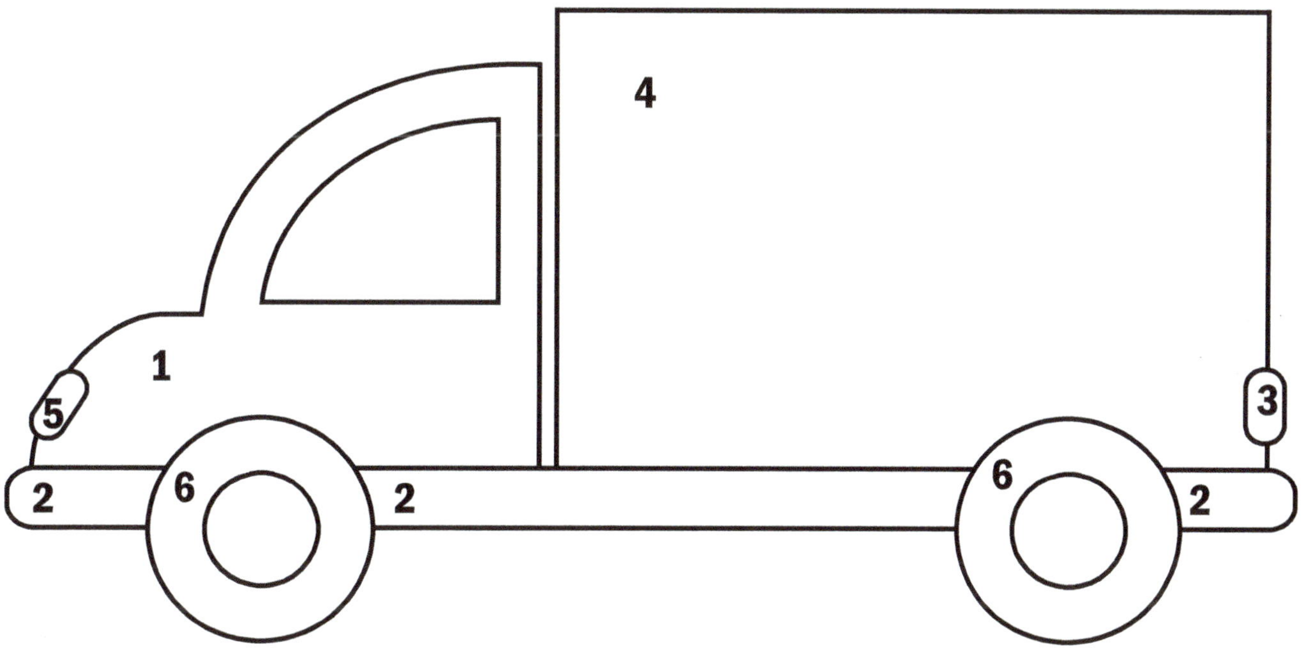

1 2 3 4 5 6

Color the picture using the code below.

1 2 3 4 5 6 7 8

Color the picture using the code below.

1 2 3 4 5 6 7 8

Color the picture using the code below.

1 2 3 4 5 6 7 8

Color the picture using the code below.

This is a Bleed Through Page If You Are Using a Coloring Marker or Pen!

Color the picture using the code below.

Color the picture using the code below.

1 2 3 4 5 6 7 8

Color the picture using the code below.

1 2 3 4 5 6 7 8

Color the picture using the code below.

1 2 3 4 5 6 7 8

Color the picture using the code below.

1 2 3 4 5 6

Color the picture using the code below.

1 2 3 4 5 6

If you love animals,
these color by number pages are sure to please.

Let's get right to it!

Color the picture using the code below.

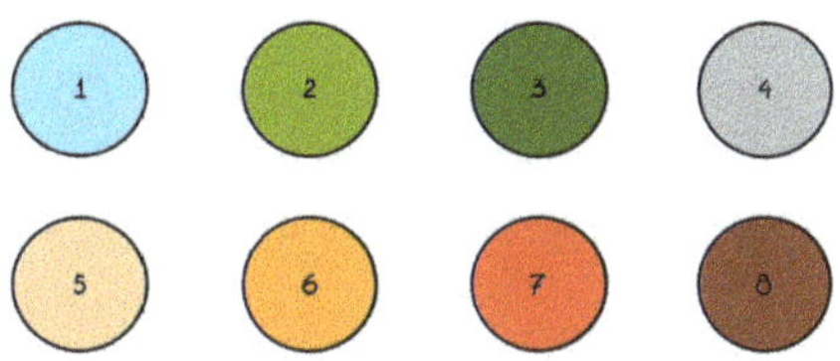

Color the picture using the code below.

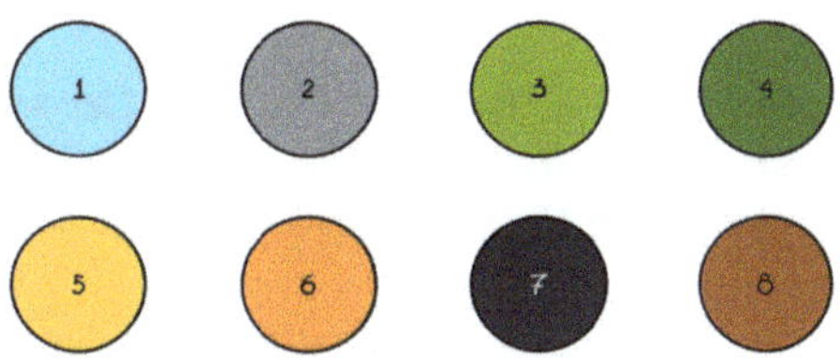

Color the picture using the code below.

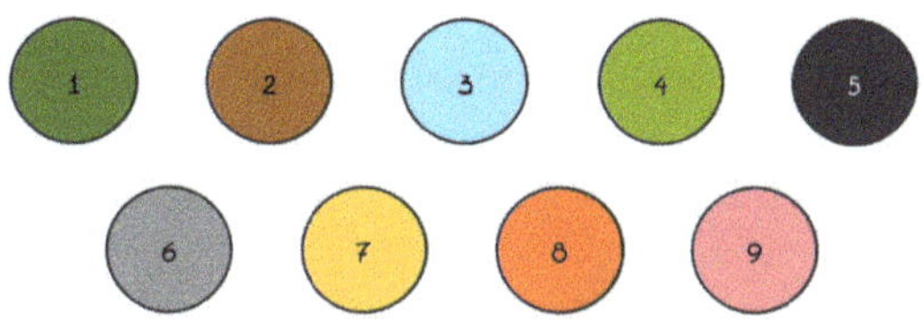

Color the picture using the code below.

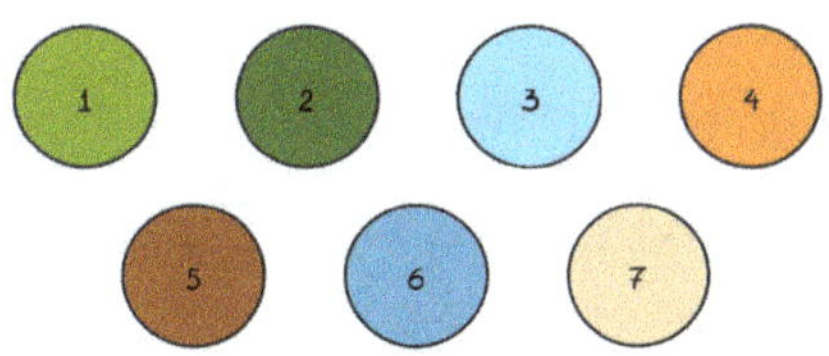

Color the picture using the code below.

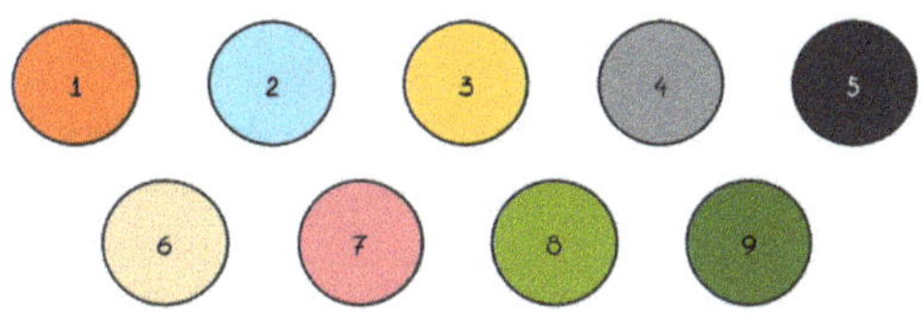

Color the picture using the code below.

1 2 3 4 5

6 7 8 9

Milton Keynes UK
Ingram Content Group UK Ltd.
UKHW051830060924
448011UK00003B/6

9 798869 418968